How to Hide a Lion

Helen Stephens

Henry Holt and Company
New York

One hot day, a lion strolled into town to buy a hat.

But the townspeople were scared of lions,

so the lion ran away.

He ran as fast and as far as he could . . .

. . . and hid in a house in a garden. It was a play house, and it belonged to a small girl called Iris.

"You can't hide there," said Iris, who wasn't scared of lions. "That house is too small for you."

They went inside so Iris could hide the lion properly. They had to be quiet because moms and dads can be funny about having a lion in the house.

The lion let Iris comb the leaves out of his mane . . .

. . . and he showed her his paw where he had stepped on something sharp. "I'll put a bandage on that," said Iris.

It wasn't easy hiding a lion. He was just too big . . .

too fluffy . . .

and too heavy, especially
when he was asleep.
And lions sleep a lot.

But when no one was looking, the lion could come out to play.

They just had to be careful
not to be too noisy.

One evening, Iris's dad said, "They still haven't found that lion."

"I bet he's a kind lion," said Iris from behind the sofa.

"There's no such thing as a kind lion," said her mom. "All lions will eat you."

The lion was worried,
but Iris comforted him.

Then she read him his favorite story. It was about a tiger who came to tea. He fell asleep halfway through, because lions sleep a lot.

And that was when everything went wrong.

Iris heard her mom
coming up the stairs,

but she found it's hard
to wake a sleeping lion.

However, most lions
will wake up if a mom
screams at them.

The lion raced out of the house . . .

. . . and found a hiding place where he could
still see Iris whenever she came into town.

Nobody noticed him.
Not the townspeople. Not even Iris.
And certainly not the two burglars who
broke into the Town Hall and stole every single
one of the mayor's candlesticks.
But the lion noticed them.

With a huge

ROAR!

he leapt off his pedestal . . .

. . . and stood on both the burglars
until the police came.

All the townspeople were amazed—except for Iris, who said, "I told you he was a kind lion."

Now the lion was a hero. He didn't have to hide anymore.
The townspeople held a special parade for him.
The mayor said he could have anything he wanted.

The lion thought for a moment.
Then he asked for . . .

. . . a hat!

Which was all he'd come to town for in the first place.

"It really suits you," said Iris.

To the Martins

Henry Holt and Company, LLC
Publishers since 1866
175 Fifth Avenue
New York, New York 10010
macKids.com

Henry Holt® is a registered trademark of Henry Holt and Company, LLC.
Copyright © 2012 by Helen Stephens
All rights reserved.

First published in 2013 in the United States by Henry Holt and Company, LLC.
Originally published in 2012 in the United Kingdom by Alison Green Books,
an imprint of Scholastic Children's Books.

Library of Congress Cataloging-in-Publication Data
Stephens, Helen, author, illustrator.
How to hide a lion / Helen Stephens. — First American edition.
pages   cm
Summary: Iris understands that grown-ups are afraid of lions, but when she finds
one in her playhouse she knows he is kind, so she keeps him hidden from her parents
for as long as possible.
ISBN 978-0-8050-9834-1 (hardcover)
[1. Lion—Fiction.] I. Title.
PZ7.S83213How 2013   [E]—dc23   2013001930

Henry Holt books may be purchased for business or promotional use. For information
on bulk purchases, please contact Macmillan Corporate and Premium Sales Department
at (800) 221-7945 x5442 or by e-mail at specialmarkets@macmillan.com.

First American Edition—2013
Printed in Singapore by Tien Wah Press Ltd.

10 9 8 7 6 5 4 3 2 1